SILK PEONY,
PARADE DRAGON

Silk Peony, Parade Dragon

by Elizabeth Steckman ✦ Illustrated by Carol Inouye

Boyds Mills Press

Published by Caroline House
Boyds Mills Press, Inc.
A Highlights Company
815 Church Street
Honesdale, Pennsylvania 18431
Printed in Mexico

Publisher Cataloging-in-Publication Data
Steckman, Elizabeth.
        Silk Peony, parade dragon / by Elizabeth Steckman ; illustrated
by Carol Inouye.—1st ed.
[32]p. : col. ill. ; cm.
Summary : How Mrs. Ming's pet dragon, Silk Peony, becomes the official
parade dragon of China.
ISBN 1-56397-233-6
1. China—Juvenile fiction. [1. China—Fiction.] I. Inouye, Carol, ill.
II. Title.
        [E]   1996   CIP
Library of Congress Catalog Card Number 94-70684

First edition, 1997
Book designed by Carol Inouye
The text of this book is set in 15-point Janson.
The illustrations are done in watercolor and gouache.

10 9 8 7 6 5 4 3 2 1

For Karen
—E. S.

For Alexandra and Peter
—C. I.

Author's Note on the Chinese New Year

The Chinese used to follow a calendar of twenty-nine or thirty days every month, based on the position of the moon. Because these lunar months do not add up to 365 days, an extra month was put in at intervals — about every sixty years. Chinese New Year can fall anytime between January 21 and February 19 by the western calendar. The years are named in groups of twelve: Rat, Ox, Tiger, Rabbit, Dragon, Snake, Horse, Sheep, Monkey, Rooster, Dog, and Boar. Every twelve years the names start over again, and each name signifies certain qualities for persons born in that year.

Mrs. Ming was so busy feeding her dragons that she did not hear the mandarin's approach.

She whirled as the ruler gave the order to lower the sedan chair until it rested on the grass.

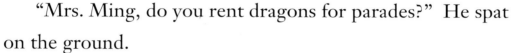

"Mrs. Ming, do you rent dragons for parades?" He spat on the ground.

Mrs. Ming didn't like to be interrupted when she was feeding her dragons, she didn't like to be surprised by four barefoot men carrying a sedan chair, and she didn't like people to spit on the ground.

Still, as upset as she was, she remembered her manners. She clasped her hands across her waist and bowed three times. "Your Excellency, I am pleased that an official as important as you should visit my humble dragon farm. Yes, I rent dragons."

Although the mandarin was the highest ruler in the province and had been placed there by the emperor himself, his manners were deplorable. "Let me see them!" he bellowed.

"I have seven dragons, Your Excellency. May I show them? . . . This one is Ling. Notice that his scales glitter like the gold of a carp. Unfortunately, he had an accident when he stumbled."

The mandarin was scornful. "He is crippled in one paw and cannot march. Why do you show him to me?"

Mrs. Ming did not answer. Instead, she bowed her head respectfully and considered another dragon.

"This one," Mrs. Ming said as she pointed to the smallest dragon, "is Jade. He was hatched in the Year of the Horse." The creature was cutting his teeth on a log.

"I don't care *when* he was hatched! He's only a puppy!"

"Our Shang has the fullest and longest beard," Mrs. Ming went on. "He certainly should have, for he is 9,763 years old. His fiery breath warms his rheumatic leg."

The mandarin pursed his lips. "A dragon with rheumatism? Bah!"

"Beside him is Han, Your Excellency. The pearl of wisdom under his chin is the size of a teacup."

"Does he lead parades?"

Mrs. Ming shook her head. "Han doesn't march, but he is the scourge of bandits."

The man's eyes glittered. "I tend to bandits in my own fashion."

Mrs. Ming pointed to another dragon. "Although Chou has the most magnificent talons, he shies at firecrackers. Shang is teaching him to accept loud noises."

The mandarin exhaled before he spoke. "A dragon that is afraid of firecrackers? Really!"

Mrs. Ming continued. "Chin, my sixth dragon, can expel his fiery breath farther than any other, but he never does so at crops or people."

"His scales are dull."

"Yes, Your Excellency. He seems to be molting."

The mandarin threw up his hands. "A scruffy lot!" he shouted. "Every one you show me is worse than the one before. And you call yourself the owner of a dragon farm? Are these *all* the miserable dragons that you have?"

Mrs. Ming remained patient. "You have seen only six dragons, Your Excellency. I have seven."

The mandarin pointed a long finger with its long fingernail
at a dragon partly hidden by a huge boulder. "Which one is that?"
"That is Silk Peony . . . . Come here, my pet, and let the
mandarin look closely at you."

The ruler sucked in his breath as he faced the most magnificent dragon he had ever seen.

As Silk Peony paced toward them, twin jets of flame came from her nostrils. She was so mannerly, however, that she held her head high and burned nothing.

The mandarin looked deep into the dragon's eyes and watched them change color from black to red. In sunlight, the dragon's scales were like the gold of a silk peony woven into the finest brocade.

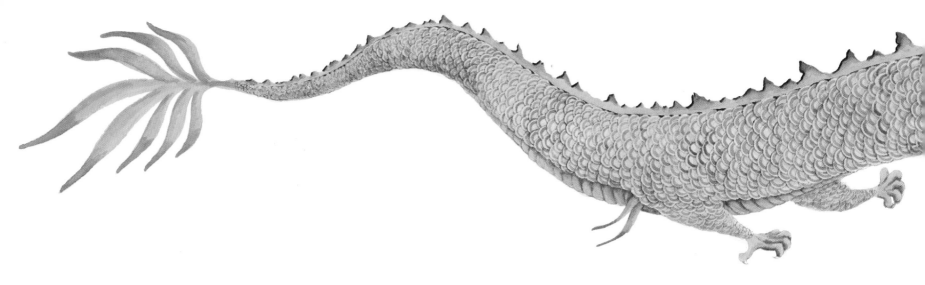

As the mandarin's mouth fell open, Mrs. Ming became worried because she believed the ruler might want Silk Peony for himself. With great effort she kept her voice calm.

"Silk Peony loves people," Mrs. Ming confided. "She is so gentle that children pat her scales."

"*She? A female* dragon?"

"Yes," Mrs. Ming explained, "She is the mother of Jade, our youngest."

The mandarin sputtered. "I need a dragon for the New Year's parade when the emperor himself comes. But a *female* dragon?"

"Please, Your Excellency, consider this dragon. She has the head of a camel, ears of a bull, eyes of a hare, mane of a lion, neck of a serpent, belly of a frog, scales of a carp, claws of an eagle, and paws of a tiger." As she spoke, Mrs. Ming counted the virtues on her fingers.

The mandarin was not convinced. "This is not a real dragon. A dragon must have the beard of a sage."

"Notice the *poh shan* on the top of her head." Mrs. Ming pointed to a kind of horn above the dragon's eyes. "The *poh shan* lets her rise to the skies."

"What do I care about a *poh shan*?" the ruler thundered. "A dragon without a beard is only a carp!"

Mrs. Ming bowed low. "Silk Peony is a *female*. Females have no beards, Your Excellency."

The mandarin was furious because the woman had spoken the truth in front of four sedan-chair bearers. He would lose face.

"Enough!" he shouted, stepping back into the sedan chair. "I will return on the fifteenth day of the next moon to select a dragon. Away!"

The sedan chair left as silently as it had come. As she watched the bearers leave, Mrs. Ming was so upset by the mandarin's rudeness that she forgot which of her dragons had been fed.

She also wondered if she should have shown her dragons to such a cruel man in the first place.

The mandarin returned on the appointed day. "Five pieces of silver to rent Silk Peony," he began.

Mrs. Ming shook her head. "Thirty, Your Excellency. Silk Peony will have to walk at least ten *li*."

The woman usually received eight silver coins for a rental, but because Chinese people love to bargain, there is never a fixed price.

"Seven pieces for your scruffy dragon."

"I might consider twenty-five for the finest dragon in China."

"You would bankrupt the province, woman. Eight pieces."

"Dragons have to eat, too, Your Excellency. Twenty pieces of silver."

"Nine pieces. Not a copper more."

"Fifteen."

"Nine."

"Fifteen."

"You drive a hard bargain, woman. Fifteen it will be."

Mrs. Ming was amazed. Never before had she rented a dragon so quickly, or for so much money.

"I will deliver Silk Peony to you the last day of the month," Mrs. Ming promised.

"And I will pay you fourteen pieces of silver."

"*Fifteen!*"

"Fifteen, then."

The last day of the old year, Mrs. Ming brought Silk Peony to the mandarin's palace.

"I would like my fifteen pieces of silver, Your Excellency."

"I am busy with the emperor, woman. I will pay you after the parade." He dismissed her with a wave of his hand.

Mrs. Ming did not wish to argue any further because the emperor might overhear her and consider her rude. She felt in her heart that not even the emperor had seen a dragon as beautiful as Silk Peony.

New Year's Day was bright and cold for the most spectacular parade in all of China. Silk Peony, with her scales shimmering gold in the winter sun, led the procession down the Street of the Bowl Makers, turned into the Street of the Silversmiths, and paced in parade step toward the Street of the Silk Weavers.

The dragon wagged her head from side to side to the beat of the drums and the shriek of the fifes. Deep rumbles came from her throat in time with the brass gongs.

Behind Silk Peony rode the emperor, smiling from his sedan chair. Even the mandarin in the chair behind the emperor nodded to the crowd and seemed pleased.

People lined the parade route fifty deep. They waved banners, tossed firecrackers, and wished the emperor, the mandarin, and each other a Happy New Year.

Children ran up to Silk Peony, patting her scales and throwing paper flowers under her paws. The elders fed her sweetmeats.

After the parade Mrs. Ming went with Silk Peony to the home of the mandarin.

"My fifteen pieces of silver, Your Excellency."

In China, all debts must be paid and all accounts settled the day before New Year. If a debt remains unpaid by daylight on New Year's Day, it has to be forgiven.

Mrs. Ming was afraid that she had waited too long.

The mandarin grinned. "It's New Year's Day, Mrs. Ming. All debts are forgiven!"

Mrs. Ming picked up a lantern from the mandarin's table.
"Will you please give me a light, Silk Peony?" she asked.

The lantern glowed with just one puff from the dragon.

"Your Excellency, if I have a lighted lantern, it is still nighttime
and New Year's Eve. Pay me my silver, sir."

"What if I don't, you miserable woman?"

"If you don't, sir, I will remind you that dragons have many
magic powers. Breathe deeply, Silk Peony, my pet."

The dragon breathed deeply, then exhaled. Her breath formed a cloud that hung from the ceiling of the palace.

"This cloud can be changed into rain or into fire, Your Excellency. Either would ruin the fine silk scrolls in this room."

"You are a bandit, woman. Begone! Servants, fan the cloud away!"

"All dragons, sir, are fond of jade and beautiful gems," Mrs. Ming went on as if the mandarin hadn't spoken. "I noticed that your chairs and tables are inlaid with both."

"I'll put you in jail!"

"And Silk Peony, also?"

For all his bluster, the mandarin was becoming frightened, for he had no wish to test the magic powers of a dragon.

"Very well. Here is your silver." And he flung a handful of silver coins on the table.

"Only fifteen, Your Excellency," said Mrs. Ming as she slid the extra coins back to the mandarin.

She bowed deeply three times before turning to the dragon. "Let's go home, Silk Peony."

The New Year's Day parade in that remote province soon became the talk of all China. Children grew up to tell their children and their children's children how Silk Peony let them pat her scales. Everyone remembered the twin jets of fire from the dragon's nostrils.

The emperor himself was so impressed that he made Silk Peony Official Parade Dragon of all China. For many generations she led the New Year's Day processions. Dragons from all over the world came to learn from the Official One.

And every year, Mrs. Ming received her fifteen pieces of silver, and no one ever tried to cheat her again.